T0396245

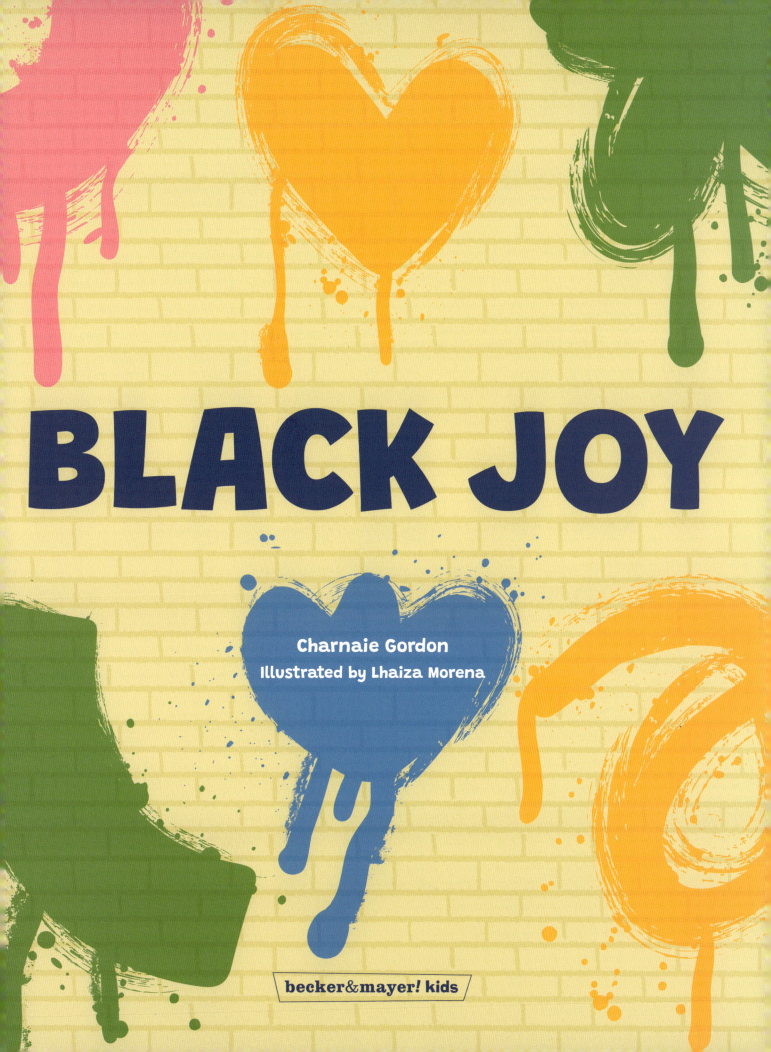

BLACK JOY

Charnaie Gordon

Illustrated by Lhaiza Morena

becker&mayer! kids

WHAT IS LOVE? Do you know?

In Jaden's west coast neighborhood, there is an old, worn-down brick wall covered in graffiti.

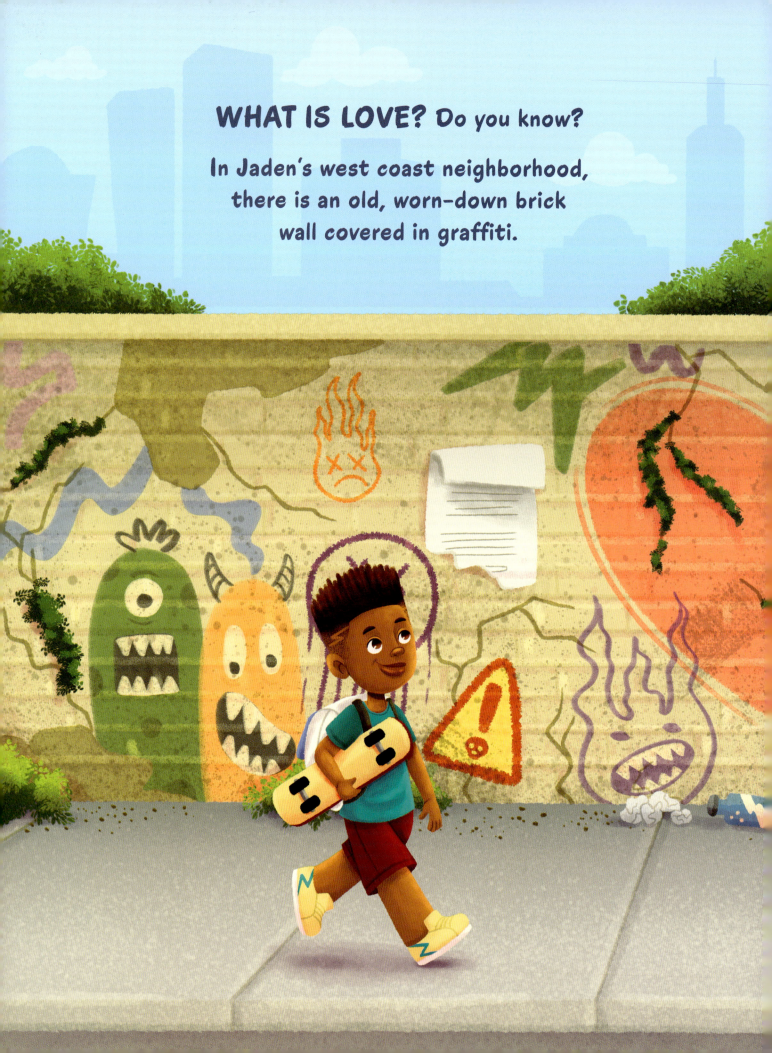

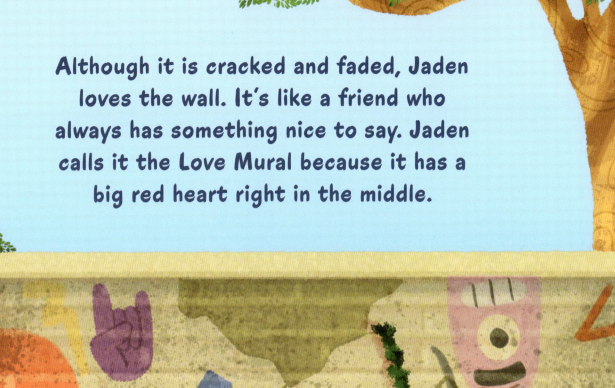

Although it is cracked and faded, Jaden loves the wall. It's like a friend who always has something nice to say. Jaden calls it the Love Mural because it has a big red heart right in the middle.

Each day on his way to
school, Jaden passes
by the Love Mural.
One day, he decides to
explore it more closely.

As Jaden touches the wall, the graffiti seems to come alive before his eyes, falling away to reveal memories of love and hope from years past.

we are love!

Feeling a special connection to
the wall, Jaden decides to make
it look beautiful again.

He'll create a new design in time for his neighborhood's annual **BLACK LOVE DAY** celebration to spread joy to everyone who sees it.

After school, Jaden tells his parents,
his sister Madison, and his brother
Jamal about his idea.

They all agree to help spread the word about the project to friends, neighbors, and other people in their community.

Jaden wants to keep the heart in the middle of the wall and add new art that shows different types of love. He writes down and draws all the ways he sees love in his life every day.

First, there's the love between his mom and dad. They start each day with hugs and kisses. They laugh, dance, and do things to make each other happy.

Jaden loves his brother and sister.

They play and sometimes argue,
but they always stick together
no matter what.

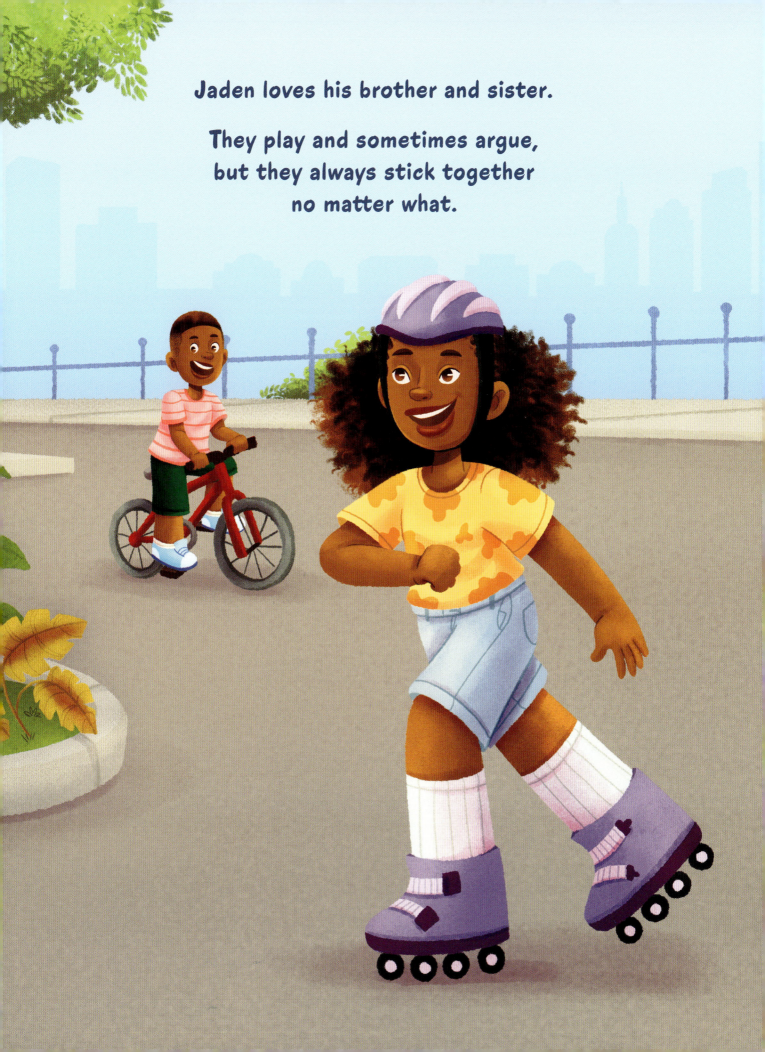

At school, Jaden is shown love
from his teacher, Mrs. Davis.

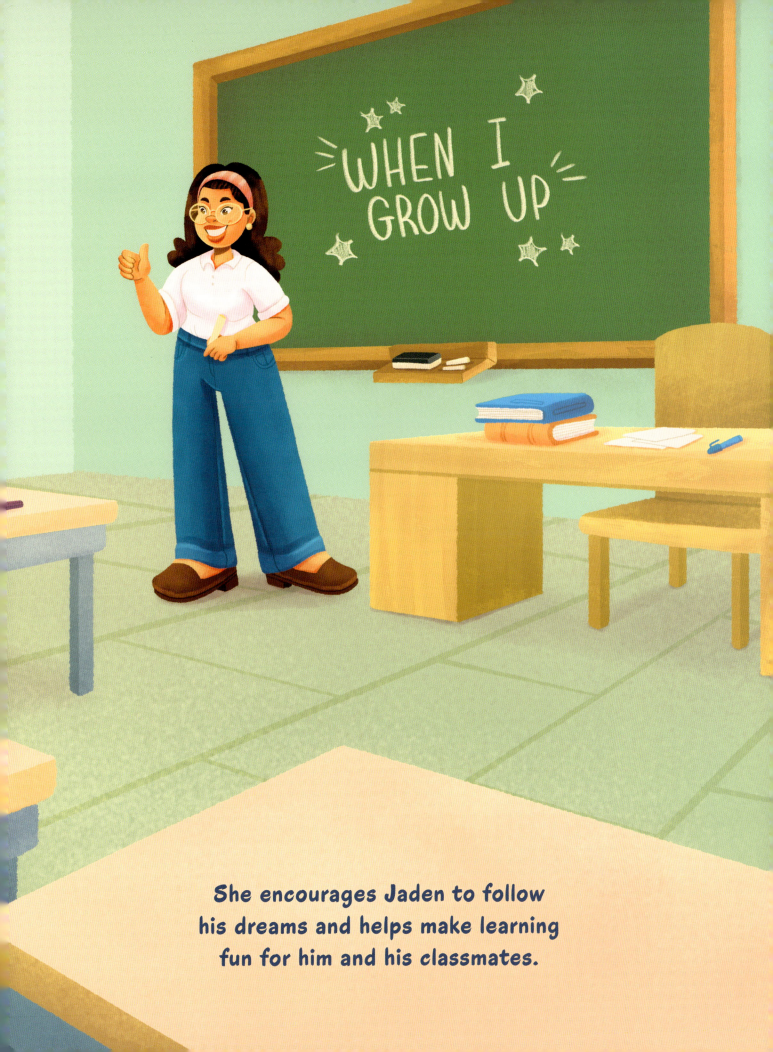

She encourages Jaden to follow his dreams and helps make learning fun for him and his classmates.

During recess, Jaden sees the love of friendship. He and his friends laugh, play, and make memories on the playground.

At Grandma and Grandpa's house,
Jaden sees the love of family history.

Jaden learns about his roots, his family's traditions, and the strength of his ancestors: all the beloved people in his family who came before him.

In his neighborhood, Jaden sees
the love of community.

His neighbors show love for Black life and culture by always being there for each other, and supporting justice, equality, and respect for everyone.

But most important is the love Jaden has for himself.

I AM STRONG, I AM SMART, AND I AM PROUD OF WHO I AM.

Jaden shares his notes and drawings for the new Love Mural with his family. They add their own ideas and ones they collected from friends and neighbors, so everyone can be a part of the mural.

Everybody pitches in and works as a
team to finish painting the new mural.
Jaden even adds his own special message
of love right next to the big red heart.

SO, WHAT IS LOVE?

Love can be shown in big and small ways. Love is more than a feeling. It is kindness, being there when people need you the most, and a choice we make every day to support one another.

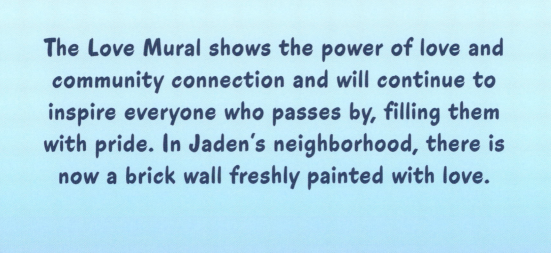

The Love Mural shows the power of love and community connection and will continue to inspire everyone who passes by, filling them with pride. In Jaden's neighborhood, there is now a brick wall freshly painted with love.

Celebrating Black Love Day

Beginning in 1993, Black Love Day is celebrated annually on February 13. The day was created to show love, forgiveness, and acceptance among Black people. Black Love Day is a healing moment for the Black community but also helps to support self-love when others try to hurt or cause harm.

While everyone knows what love is, Black Love Day is about celebrating Black culture through these five themes:

1. LOVE TOWARD THE CREATOR
2. LOVE TOWARD SELF
3. LOVE TOWARD FAMILY
4. LOVE WITHIN THE BLACK COMMUNITY
5. LOVE FOR THE BLACK RACE

The goal is to practice these ideas in your everyday life throughout the year but to show Black Love the most on February 13 while celebrating all the wonderful parts of Black culture.

Show your Black joy in how you love yourself, your family, and your community!

Black Love Day Activities

Memory Jar

You will need:

+ 1 16-oz Mason jar
+ Paintbrush (e.g., Mr. Pen)
+ Spray paint, chalk paint, or acrylic paint in red, black, and green colors
+ Additional items to decorate with, like ribbon, stickers, or glitter (optional)
+ Craft glue (e.g., Aleene's All Purpose Tacky Glue)
+ Scissors
+ Writing paper cut into strips
+ Pens or pencils

Step 1: Paint the Mason jar with red, black, and green paint in any fun design you choose. If decorating with additional items, attach with craft glue (if needed) once the paint has dried.

Step 2: Cut paper into small strips with enough room for writing.

Step 3: Write down your favorite memories of moments when you have felt loved, supported, or proud to be Black.

Step 4: Fill the jar with the memory notes and read them together as a family on Black Love Day, reflecting on the strength and beauty of Black love and culture.

Happy Thoughts Bracelets

You will need:

+ 6 mm-sized plastic or gemstone beads in colors representing African heritage (red, green, black, gold)
+ 6 mm-sized plastic beads with letters of the alphabet on them
+ 33 ft (10 m) spool of 1-mm- or .08-mm-wide stretchy elastic cord
+ for jewelry making (e.g., Konmay, Paxcoo, Stretch Magic) or pipe cleaners in your choice of colors
+ Scissors

Important to remember:

+ The size or length of a bracelet usually depends on three things: 1) the size of the person or wearer's wrist, 2) the size of the beads, and 3) the style of the beaded bracelet.
+ Larger wood beads or pony beads can be used with smaller children. Beads may be a choking hazard for smaller children so parental supervision is advised.
+ Pipe cleaners are easier to string beads onto and can be used for younger children in place of the elastic cord.

Step 1: Measure the wrist of the person you are making the bracelet for with a piece of elastic cord or pipe cleaners by wrapping it around their wrist.

Step 2: Use a marker to mark where the bracelet will end or close. The bracelet can be tight or loose, whatever fits best, but include a little extra to make stringing the beads easy.

Step 3: Cut the length that you need.

Step 4: Choose the letter beads you need to spell out positive sayings or words like "I am loved," "Strong," "I am enough," or "Brave."

Step 5: Choose a selection of beads in your favorite colors. The number of colored beads will depend on the length of the word or saying you choose.

Step 6: Decide on the design or pattern you would like to create for your bracelet before you start stringing the beads. Lay the beads out on the table in front of you in the order you want them to appear on the bracelet, from left to right.

Step 7: Starting from the left, string the beads onto the elastic cord or pipe cleaners.

Step 8: When you've finished stringing the beads, tie the elastic cord with a good, strong knot to secure the beads, or twist the free ends of the pipe cleaner together.

Step 9: Cut off any extra elastic cord or pipe cleaner with scissors.

Step 10: Wear your bracelet as a reminder of self-love and all the great things that you can do!

About the Author

Charnaie Gordon is a diversity and inclusion advocate, podcast host, and digital creator. She is also the author of the picture books *Lift Every Voice and Change*, *Heroic Heart*, *A Kids Book About Diversity*, and many more. Charnaie's blog, *Here Wee Read*, is where she expresses her creativity and passion for reading, diverse literature, and literacy. She's also the founder of her children's literacy nonprofit organization, 50 States 50 Books, Inc., that collects and donates diverse children's books to deserving kids in each of the fifty US states. She lives in Connecticut with her husband and two children.

About the Illustrator

Born and raised in Bahia, Brazil, **Lhaiza Morena** graduated with a degree in computer graphics and has worked as an art director in advertising agencies. Since 2018 she has worked in the area of illustration with a focus on children's books, character design, and advertising, bringing Black representation whenever possible and illustrating with bright colors and textures.

First published in 2025 by becker&mayer!kids, an imprint of The Quarto Group,
142 West 36th Street, 4th Floor, New York, NY 10018, USA
(212) 779-4972 www.Quarto.com

becker&mayer!kids titles are also available at discount for retail, wholesale, promotional, and bulk purchase. For details, contact the Special Sales Manager by email at specialsales@quarto.com or by mail at The Quarto Group, Attn: Special Sales Manager, 100 Cummings Center Suite 265D, Beverly, MA 01915, USA.

10 9 8 7 6 5 4 3 2

ISBN: 978-0-7603-9439-7

Digital edition published in 2025
eISBN: 978-0-7603-9441-0

Library of Congress Cataloging-in-Publication Data

Names: Gordon, Charnaie, author. | Morena, Lhaiza illustrator.
Title: Black joy / Charnaie Gordon ; Illustrated by Lhaiza Morena.
Description: New York, NY : becker&mayer!kids, an imprint of The Quarto
   Group, 2025. | Audience: Ages 6-11. | Audience: Grades K-1. | Summary:
   African American Jaden celebrates Black Love Day by designing a mural
   for his neighborhood that reflects all the love in his community.
Identifiers: LCCN 2024027726 (print) | LCCN 2024027727 (ebook) | ISBN
   9780760394397 (hardcover) | ISBN 9780760394403 (paperback) | ISBN
   9780760394410 (ebook) | ISBN 9780760394427 (ebook)
Subjects: CYAC: Mural painting and decoration--Fiction. |
   Communities--Fiction. | Love--Fiction. | African Americans--Fiction. |
   LCGFT: Picture books.
Classification: LCC PZ7.1.G654585 Bl 2025 (print) | LCC PZ7.1.G654585
   (ebook) | DDC [E]--dc23
LC record available at https://lccn.loc.gov/2024027726
LC ebook record available at https://lccn.loc.gov/2024027727

Group Publisher: Rage Kindelsperger
Creative Director: Laura Drew
Managing Editor: Cara Donaldson
Cover and Interior Design: Scott Richardson
Illustrations: Lhaiza Morena

Printed in China

LEXILE

Lexile® 860L

MIX
Paper | Supporting responsible forestry
FSC® C016973